For more than forty years,
Yearling has been the leading name
in classic and award-winning literature
for young readers.

Yearling books feature children's
favorite authors and characters,
providing dynamic stories of adventure,
humor, history, mystery, and fantasy.

Trust Yearling paperbacks to entertain,
inspire, and promote the love of reading
in all children.

THE FUTURE
IS NOW!

Read all the Time Surfers books:

SPACE BINGO
ORBIT WIPEOUT!
MONDO MELTDOWN
INTO THE ZONK ZONE!
SPLASH CRASH!
ZERO HOUR
SHOCK WAVE
DOOM STAR

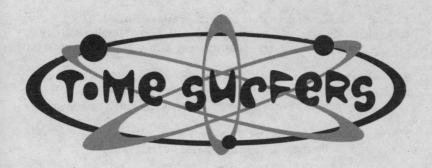

INTO THE ZONK ZONE!

ILLUSTRATED BY KIM MULKEY

A YEARLING BOOK

Published by Yearling, an imprint of Random House Children's Books
a division of Random House, Inc., New York

Visit us on the Web! www.randomhouse.com/kids

Educators and librarians, for a variety of teaching tools,
visit us at www.randomhouse.com/teachers

ISBN: 978-0-553-48307-9

Printed in the United States of America

Originally published by Bantam Skylark in 1996

First Yearling Edition August 2008

11 10 9 8 7 6 5 4 3 2

For Wendy Loggia,
my most excellent surfie partner
on this wild ride

CHAPTER
✳ 1 ✳

"It'll go like clockwork!" Ned Banks said into his personal communicator. "No problem."

Ned had been through it all a thousand times. He knew exactly how it would work.

"I get to school early," he said, leaning back on his bed and staring at the ceiling. "It's totally deserted, no one around. I slip into the gym, up to the stage, and into the timehole behind the curtain."

"Cool," came the response from the little black device in Ned's hand. It was the voice of his best friend, Ernie Somers, a thousand miles away in his own room. "Then what?"

1

Ned smiled at the next part. "I hop in my surfie and blast over to your house at a hundred miles a second!"

"Awesome!" Ernie said. "Can you pull it off without Mr. Smott catching you?"

Ned looked over at the big backpack sitting on his desk. It was stuffed with homework due the next day—the last day of school. His teacher, Mr. Smott, didn't seem to like Ned very much. He always frowned and sent notes home.

Worse than that, Mr. Smott always seemed to be around when Ned was near a timehole.

"Hey, what could happen? It's the last day of school. Of course I can pull it off. I'm a Time Surfer!"

Ned Banks was an official Time Surfer. With Roop Johnson and Suzi Naguchi, his friends from the year 2099, Ned traveled in time doing absolutely amazing things.

Ned even had his own bright yellow time-traveling surfie. For the past few weeks it had been stuck in the timehole in the gym. He had to get it out of there.

2

"When you get here I'll show you the brand-new foil-embossed 3-D Zontar card," Ernie said. "Ned, the dude is awesome!" Ned and Ernie collected every Zontar comic, card, milk cap, and action figure.

"See you in the morning, Ern." Ned switched off the device and turned out his bedroom light. *Like clockwork*, he thought. *No problem.*

But when Ned walked up to the front of Lakewood School the next morning, with the sun just creeping over the roof of the gym, it didn't seem like no problem.

It seemed like—big problem!

Hundreds of students and teachers and parents were swarming all over the school. The parking lot was filled with moms and dads dropping off their kids.

"But, what—what—how—" stammered Ned, twisting his Indians cap from front to back. "It's only seven-thirty. The school should be deserted!"

"The only thing that's deserted is your brain, *Nerd*," a voice said.

Ned whirled around. He knew that voice too well. It was his snotty sister, Carrie. She always called him Nerd.

"What are you doing here?" Ned asked, confused. He couldn't figure it out.

"Pretty dorky to be late the last day of school," Carrie said, ignoring his question. "Or did you forget the big concert? You were supposed to be here early to practice your part. Wake up, tuba boy."

"Huh?"

"Knock knock. Earth to Ned. Don't you know what time it is?" She flashed a fake smile, tapped her saxophone case, and ran to join her friends.

Time? thought Ned. Of course he knew what time it was. He knew more about time than anyone in the whole school. He traveled in time. He studied time. He knew everything about time, from when it started with a big—

Bang! The front door of the school flew open and a figure stormed out, frowning a terrible frown at Ned and tapping his watch.

"Mr. Smott!" Ned gasped. "Oh no! I'm late

4

for band rehearsal!" Ned was supposed to be rehearsing his part for the last-day concert, the big event of the year. He grabbed his backpack, made his way through the crowd, and hustled in the front door of the school.

Mr. Smott stomped across the hall toward the gym on Ned's heels.

Ned knew Mr. Smott hated directing the band. The real band teacher was having a baby. Mr. Smott had been asked to fill in.

Ned passed the open doors of the cafeteria. Mrs. Fensterman, the coach's wife, was helping a bunch of mothers and teachers decorate tables for the reception after the concert. Plates of cookies and brownies and piles of yellow napkins were everywhere.

"I told you before, son," Mrs. Fensterman said as Ned passed by. "Don't touch. It's all for later."

"Told me before?" Ned made a face. He looked over at the tables. Lemonade. Soda. Cookies. Brownies. It looked so normal.

It wasn't.

What Mrs. Fensterman didn't know—what nobody knew except Ned—was that a few feet away, in the kitchen's giant refrigerator, was a shimmering timehole to the future!

There were timeholes all over Lakewood School. In the janitor's supply closet. Behind the bleachers. On the stage in the gym.

Timeholes were everywhere. Ned even had a timehole in his bedroom.

But you had to have a special device to be able to find timeholes. A device that Ned had invented.

In fact, that was how it had all started. One night, just after Ned had moved to Lakewood, he'd been alone in his room making a super-long-distance communicator, a device he planned to use to call Ernie back in Newton Falls.

He'd made it with an old TV remote, some junk from a tape recorder, buzzers, lights, and other stuff.

But something had gone wrong. Instead of reaching Ernie, Ned had opened a timehole in his closet and beamed in two kids from the future!

"Banks, hurry up!" Mr. Smott called, pointing up at the clock on the wall.

Ned dashed for the music room next to the gym. He grabbed his big, heavy, monster tuba and ran back through the doors into the gym.

Bong! Ned tripped. The tuba sprang back at him, and he tumbled to the floor with his head in the mouth of the huge instrument.

This happened just as his sister and her friends came into the gym. They stood over him.

"See what I mean?" Carrie said.

Ned pulled his head out of the tuba and swept past them to the stage, stopping in the back row of chairs.

He glanced at a patch of floor behind the curtain. It *looked* like a regular wooden floor. But the moment he hit a button on his communicator—*whoosh!*—a blazing blue timehole would appear there, just the way it did that first night in his room.

Tap-tap-tap. Mr. Smott hit the music stand in front of him. "Well, since you're all here now, let's begin with 'The March of the Soldiers.' "

The teacher frowned, raised his arms, and quickly began to swing them up and down.

Bump-a-dump-a-dump-a—Floook! Floook! The band began squealing and screeching and got worse with each note. It was all saxophones except for Ned. And he was the worst. Every time he blew into that tuba, it sounded like a cow with a bad stomachache.

"Stop!" cried Mr. Smott. "Stop this instant!"

He stormed from the stage to the gym floor. "Saxophones, down here!" he snarled.

Twenty kids rushed down the stairs with their saxophones, leaving Ned and his tuba onstage.

"Um, Mr. Smott?" said Ned, tapping his tuba.

"I'll deal with you later!" Mr. Smott barked.

Good, thought Ned. This was his chance. He slipped behind the curtain. "Ernie," he whispered to himself, "I'm on my way!"

That was the great thing about time travel. Ned could zip off to some cool place, have a great time all day, then come back to the exact second he'd left and nobody would even know!

The only problem was something called the Zonk Zone. Two people in the same place and time—that was the Zonk Zone. Ned had nearly been zonked once already. It wasn't fun.

He pulled his communicator from his backpack, aimed it, and pressed the green button.

Whoosh!—a silvery blue ring of light fluttered open on the stage floor. Beyond the ring of light a tunnel shimmered off into the darkness.

A timehole! Ned never got over the strange excitement of staring at an entrance into time. In an instant he'd be at Ernie's house, spend an hour joking around, and then—bingo!—be back before Mr. Smott had moved an inch.

He'd still have to play his tuba, but it was cool knowing he could see Ernie anytime he wanted.

Timeholes were excellent!

Ned jumped down through the blue ring, below the floor of the stage, and out of time.

There it was. His beautiful yellow surfie with blue fins arching up the back. It was sleek and superfast. Ned's little secret.

"But," Ned muttered, walking around the ship. Something was different. Something was wrong. The surfie wasn't where he'd left it. And the jets on the back looked like they'd been fired recently. "Someone's been here!"

Suddenly Ned heard a noise behind him. He glanced up to see the thick red curtains ripple, sway, and swing apart.

A face stared down into the timehole.

"No!" cried Ned.

CHAPTER
* 2 *

"Afterburners—on!" yelled Ned.

A burst of flame shot out the back of the little ship, sending a jet of fiery air up and out of the timehole.

An instant later Ned was gone, hurtling through the silvery blue timehole at incredible speed. The sides of the tunnel blurred. His face felt as if it was being pulled back into a silly grin. "That was way too close!" he said, setting the controls for Ernie's house.

Suddenly—*diddle-iddle-eep! Eep!* His communicator began to sound.

"Oh, no! It's Roop and Suzi, calling from the future! Sorry, Ernie," he muttered. "Our summer kickoff is going to have to wait. Future, here I come!"

He reset the surfie's controls and focused on the communicator's little screen. In the future everybody had a communicator like Ned's. In fact, they were called Neddies!

The years ticked by. A moment later the timehole dissolved around him.

The year—2099!

The place—Mega City!

Mega City! Vast metropolis of thousands of buildings, millions of lights, tens of millions of people. Tall towers soared up from the ground.

Mega City was home to Roop and Suzi and the incredible world of the Time Surfers.

Ned dipped the surfie under the Sky Rink, a floating stadium where kids played bloogball, the official game of the future.

The year 2099 was an amazing time. The motto was—*kids rule!*

But it wasn't always that way.

Not long ago, Ned and Ernie had discovered a different, frightening future. Mega

City wasn't Mega City and Earth wasn't Earth.

And it was all because of one person. One creature. *Vorg!* The name made Ned tremble.

Ned leaned over the side and spotted Spider Base, the official home of the Time Surfers. He pushed the control stick down.

Suddenly a shadow passed over his surfie.

"Intruder alert! Intruder alert!" roared a loud robotic voice in the skies behind him.

"Wha—" Ned turned to see a large cone-shaped flying ship closing in fast from above. A silver arm with a giant claw on the end shot out from the ship's great hull.

"Hey!" shouted Ned, trying to dip his surfie out of the way. "I'm a Time—"

Klong! The claw clamped fast on the surfie. Ned's engine suddenly went dead.

Rrrrr! The giant cone shot forward, the tip spiraled open, and—*ka-thung!*—it closed around the surfie like a set of jaws.

Ned began to sweat.

A moment later the ship landed with a thud.

Rrrrr! The tip of the cone spiraled open slowly. Bright light flooded the chamber.

Standing in front of the light was a figure. Ned couldn't see its face. He could only make out its shape.

It moved toward him.

Ned could almost hear the deep, gravelly voice beginning to speak.

There was no place to run.

"Stop!" Ned cried out. "Get away from me!"

The figure stopped and tilted its head. "Dude, is that you?"

"Huh?" said Ned.

The figure snapped its fingers and waved its hand in a "Hi" motion. The official Time Surfer salute! "Hey, I do believe it's the Nedmeister!"

Ned couldn't believe his ears. "Roop?"

Flink! Lights went on in the cone. Stepping into the opening was a kid dressed in a silver Time Surfer flight suit. His hair was cut into a flattop with zigzags on the sides.

It was Roop Johnson!

"You!" said Ned. "I thought I was doomed!"

"Sorry about the weird reception committee," said Roop, tapping the cone's nose. "But we've got a very strange mystery on our hands. Let's get to the dome and I'll show you."

Ned followed Roop out of the cone into a large gray room. He recognized it right away as one of the hangars in Spider Base.

Kids and grown-ups in different-colored flight suits were scrambling everywhere around him.

"Ned!" shouted a girl from across the room. She ran over.

It was Suzi Naguchi, the third member of TS Squad One. She had a pair of goggles pushed up on her forehead, and her short black hair was tucked behind her ears.

"I just finished my homework!" she said, holding out a hand for Ned and Roop to see. In her palm was a small pile of black dust.

"What was your assignment, make dirt?" asked Ned, making a face.

Suzi laughed. "This dust used to be one of those." She pointed to a large metal canister that held fuel for rocket flights.

Ned's eyes went wide. "But how—"

"Zonk Zone. I artificially created a Zone in the lab to see if I could find a way to get rid of trash. I sent one of those canisters back in time to the same place and time it already was. There was, uh, sort of an explosion."

Ned stared at the black dust. "Sort of?"

"Zonk-o-rama!" Roop exclaimed. "That's the thing about time travel. Can be fun, could be deadly."

Ned nodded. "I gotta remind myself not to get anywhere near me, no matter when I am."

Suzi laughed again, brushed the dust into a bag, and headed with the two boys to the dome.

Suddenly Roop stopped and stared at a metal door closing in front of them. "My feet can't help themselves!" he cried.

Roop dropped to his knees and flicked a switch on each shoe.

Whoom! Flames roared from the backs of Roop's shoes. He leaned back and powered under the door just before it closed.

"He's a nut," said Ned.

Suzi rolled her eyes. "Yeah, I wonder where he gets it from."

Fwang! The metal door shot up, and there was Roop, lying on the floor with his hands under his head, grinning like an imp. "I just can't resist the call of the door."

Suzi tucked her goggles into her pocket and stepped over Roop into the dome, the control room and teaching lab of Spider Base. On the ceiling was a giant screen. A 3-D video was being shown.

It was a surfie. A yellow surfie. Ned's own surfie, shooting all over Mega City, nearly colliding with every building in the skyline!

"What's going on?" Ned cried. "I'm not a great flyer, but I'm not *that* bad."

"We figured it wasn't you," Roop said, scratching the zigzags above his ears.

Ned gasped and ducked as his surfie nearly crashed into the top of the very dome they were now standing in. "Who's flying it? My surfie's a secret."

Roop turned some dials at the video control podium, trying to get a better focus. "We couldn't get the cameras close enough before the surfie vanished."

Ned was quiet for a while. He remembered the timehole under the stage. His surfie had been moved. Someone had been using it.

Suzi put her hand on his shoulder. "Your secret isn't secret anymore."

Vrrrr! A door on the far side of the dome slid up, and a woman strode in. She wore a sparkly white space suit.

Ned recognized her as Commander Nara Johnson, Roop's mother. She greeted Ned with a snap wave as she walked over to them.

"Ned, we try to keep time travel under control. Unfortunately, someone from your time has discovered its secret. You'll have to be careful."

Ned nodded to the commander. "I'm going to move my surfie to my closet the first

chance I get. So maybe we'll be okay." He looked at his friends. "I hope."

Roop started waving his arms up and down. "Can we tell him, Mom?"

Suzi beamed. "Can we, Commander? Please?"

"Tell me what?" asked Ned, puzzled.

"Krono City!" Roop blurted out. "Oops!" He looked over at his mother. She laughed.

"Ned," said Commander Johnson, "today is a special day. Thirty years ago this very day, the Time Surfers began."

"Time Surfers!" sang Roop. "Our mission is—one, to help people!"

"Two," said Suzi, "to keep the galaxy healthy."

"Three," Ned added, "to have fun wherever we go!"

Commander Johnson nodded. "We're celebrating with a ceremony at Krono City, the scene of the last battle of the shadow wars, when the Time Surfers first defeated Vorg."

"Too bad he didn't stay defeated," said Ned.

"We're also celebrating the way you kids saved the world," Commander Johnson added. "Vorg's horrible future almost became real. Luckily, you stopped him."

"Thirty years ago! Can you believe our parents were actually *alive* back then?" Suzi asked.

Roop nodded. "It was the battle of the century. Even if it happened so long ago."

Commander Johnson frowned. "It wasn't that long ago, you two!" She started for the launch hangar.

"Slide, Mom!" Roop called out, laughing, as she approached the door.

"I don't do that!" Commander Johnson said as the door went up. "Anymore."

Thunk! The door closed behind her.

"Krono City is the ultimate in cool, Nedman!" said Roop. "And the best part is—it's on the moon!"

"You'll love it, Ned. Look!" Suzi sprinted over to the control platform in the dome's center and hit a button. Instantly the dome showed a picture of Krono City, a vast station of many towers on the moon's surface.

"Built right on the site of the final battle. It's one of the zommoest places in the galaxy," Roop said. "Ultimate for vacations. They have Zoofi Cones, jetters, the solar system's biggest Flinch Smasher, a Wonk Tube—"

"Huh?"

"Never mind, you'll have a blast!"

"And," added Suzi, "we can take a side trip to the place where people first landed!"

"Wow!" Ned blinked. "Me? On the moon?"

Roop slapped him on the back. "Don't worry, dude, you can leave the flying to us."

"Yeah, but—"

"No buts, Ned! You're a Time Surfer. It's a special day for all Time Surfers!" Suzi told him. "Besides, if you hadn't stopped that megacomet from destroying Earth, we'd probably all be speaking Klenn now!"

"Saying things like *'Bocka-wocka-Vorg!'* " Roop quipped. "Or *'Cho-lo-bo-lo, Klenn-o!'* "

Ned shivered, remembering the strange Klenn language used in the Zontar comic books. A language that the actual Klenn holodroids used in the future.

23

Ned gazed at the peaceful moon station on the ceiling. He couldn't believe that it had once been the scene of the fiercest of battles.

Then, as he looked up at the giant blue dome, Krono City's bright towers and floating globes began to grow dim.

"What's happening?" said Suzi, adjusting the controls.

Before anyone could answer, the image of Krono City quivered, blinked—and disappeared! In its place were the charred craters and desolate mountains of the moon!

"Krono City!" cried Roop in astonishment. "It's—it's gone!"

CHAPTER ✳ 3 ✳

Weee-oooop! Weee-oooop!

Alarms sounded throughout Spider Base.

"It's impossible!" said Suzi, running for the launch room. She pulled out her Neddy and flipped on the screen. "No way!"

As Ned ran, a word came tumbling out of his mouth. A single word. A name.

"Vorg."

"What?" asked Roop.

"Vorg," Ned repeated without taking a breath. "He's doing this. He's messing with time."

Suzi rounded a corner and dashed into the landing bay, staring at her Neddy. "Vector search says that Krono City hasn't existed for thirty years! That can't be! We just saw it!"

"Vorg is changing the past," said Ned. "He wants his horrible future and won't stop until he gets it. Just like he tried before."

A look of horror crept over Roop's face. "Thirty years? That means Krono City was never built. It means that Vorg *won* the shadow wars!"

Alarms sounded down every corridor of Time Surfer headquarters. Kids were all over the place, running down the halls, pulling on strange flight equipment.

Ned thought about what Roop had said. "Listen, guys. On our last mission we discovered Vorg's future and we changed it back. Now he's doing it again by changing history. Vorg City, Vorgon, the whole Vorg universe!"

Suzi was quiet for a long time. Finally she said, "We have to go back. Thirty years ago. To the final battle on the moon. We have to make sure it happens the right way."

Roop nodded. "A mission for Time Surfer Squad One."

Ned knew they were right. "Let's go!"

Suzi raced over to a nearby closet and yanked it open. On a hanger was a brand-new silver suit. A tag taped to it read NED BANKS. SIZE 10.

"Here," said Suzi, ripping off the tag and thrusting the suit at Ned. "We were saving this for later, but there's no time."

"Wow," said Ned, fingering the shiny fabric.

"Don't forget your speed shoes!" Roop added, tossing him a pair.

In a flash they were standing by their surfies. Dozens of other Time Surfers were standing at attention, too.

Commander Johnson and Commander Naguchi, Suzi's father, hurried over. "Each surfie is equipped with personal jet packs and a stunner," Commander Naguchi informed them.

"A stunner?" Ned asked.

"An awesome device," explained Roop.

"Blast an alien and he hangs there frozen in time until you blast him again."

"Sounds great for Klenn-busting," Ned said.

"Where you're going, you'll need them," said Commander Johnson.

"But what about air?" asked Ned. "Where are our helmets?"

"This is 2099!" said Roop. "Our suits are equipped with projectrodes. They create an oxygen shield all around us."

"Cool," said Ned, checking the little knobs on the shoulders of his flight suit. He turned to Commander Naguchi. "Is going back thirty years, you know, safe?"

"At least we won't see ourselves!" said Roop. "We're Zonk Zone free!"

Commander Naguchi flashed a look at Roop's mother. She took a deep breath. "Well, that's true, but you might find . . . uh . . ." She stopped. "Just be careful."

"Come on, let's blast!" said Suzi. "There's no telling what else Vorg is up to!"

Suzi hugged and kissed her father, and Roop did the same with his mother.

"Cool, we're on a mission!" exclaimed Roop.

"But don't forget, son," his mother said. "You still have to clean your room tonight."

"Oh, man! Kids really *do* do everything!" Roop grumbled.

Along with everyone else, they tightened their belts and climbed into their surfies. In a moment the two small ships, one purple, one yellow, followed by a dozen other surfies, zoomed from Spider Base, shot into a dark timehole, and tunneled back in time.

"A Time Surfer mission," Ned said to himself. "To save the future! And the past!" As he worked the controls of his surfie, the screen on his control panel turned from black to blue. Roop's face appeared. "Hey, Ned dude, remember to watch out for hinge-wings and roachbacks." Roop cut off, and the screen went black.

Ned stared into his screen. "Hey, you can't say that and then just hang up!"

Suzi's face appeared. "Hinge-wings," she said, "are robot air fighters. And roachbacks are armored ground rovers. There were lots of them during the shadow wars."

"Oh," said Ned, steering his ship through a series of S-turns in the time tunnel.

An instant later the surfies jumped from the timehole and skimmed just inches above a desert of sandy gray soil.

"Bitzo, is this it?" Ned asked his surfie's onboard computer. "Is this the moon?"

The computer hummed to life. "Vector co-ordinates indicate proximity to surface terrain of terrestrial orbiting planetoidal body."

Ned made a face, steering the surfie over a ridge of gray rock. "Um . . . what?"

"The moon," droned Bitzo.

"Thanks for the translation!" Ned scanned the sky above him. It was dark, calm, nighttime. Pulling up alongside him was the nose of the purple surfie. Inside the bubble top he saw Suzi working the flight controls. Roop was strapping on his stunner. On the strap was the great Time Surfer emblem.

Behind the two lead surfies was a fleet of Time Surfers in their surfies.

"This is incredible," said Ned. "Here we are in our own spaceships, in the year 2069! Fighting the forces of evil in one wicked moon battle!"

"Yeah," chuckled Roop from Ned's screen. "I'd love to hear you say that when Mr. Smott asks why you're late."

"Oh, thanks," Ned snapped. "You had to remind me!"

A thin band of light shined up ahead as the surfies approached the light side of the moon. It seemed incredible, all right. And yet, if Ned and his friends couldn't bring back Krono City, the future would be changed forever.

As they rose over a low range of hills and into the light, Ned caught sight of it for the first time.

A great blue ball with swirling white patches on it, floating out in the darkness of space.

"Earth!" he gasped. "Home!"

It was then that he realized the magnitude of what he and his friends had to do in the next few minutes.

32

"Save Earth!" he said.

"That's what it's all about," said Suzi from the screen in front of Ned.

As they headed toward a crater below, red lightning blasted across the sky.

Suddenly there they were! The hinge-wings! Five black robot air fighters sliced through the smoky air, turning sharp circles as they dived toward the little surfies.

They were very fast.

"Robots control them!" shouted Roop, his hands gripping his surfie's laser guns. "They never miss!"

"Who controls the robots?" shouted Ned.

Roop shot him a look. "Vorg!"

The huge steel birds flashed across the sky and opened fire!

CHAPTER
* 4 *

KA-BLAM—BLAM—BLAM!

Blast after blast of fiery red lightning cut through the darkness, scattering the fleet of surfies in all directions.

Ned slammed his control stick forward and dived straight for the ground as the flash exploded near him.

When he dived, he saw two kids in blue space suits and helmets running up the side of a crater trying to escape the hinge-wings' laser fire.

"Guys!" cried Ned into the screen. "We've got to get down there right away. Those kids are in danger!"

"If Vorg wins this battle," said Roop, "we're *all* in danger!"

"Let's do it!" cried Suzi.

Both surfies circled and skidded to a stop on the dusty surface. Ned grabbed the small tube-shaped jet pack and snapped it onto his belt. He pulled a stunner from its holder, popped up the bubble on his surfie, and jumped out.

Vlaaam! A hinge-wing fired one last shot just as the two kids in blue helmets leaped over the rim. Ned watched them run, drop to their knees, and slide down the inside crater wall. "Cool! The first Time Surfers! And they already know how to slide!"

The black robot fighters veered back to the battle zone.

Roop and Suzi ran over to join Ned as he reached the two kids, but the moment they got there, they froze.

"Who . . . ," said Roop.

"Who . . . ," said Suzi.

One was a boy, the other a girl. The girl looked at Ned. "Your friends seem human, but they talk like owls. My name is Nara."

"Nara," repeated Ned, helping her up. "Hey, Roop, she has the same name as—"

"I know!" Roop dived over and locked his hand across Ned's mouth.

The girl raised her eyebrows. "My friend here is—"

"Zeno!" Suzi blurted out.

"Wow!" said the boy next to her. "How'd you know that?"

"Uh . . . lucky guess," Suzi mumbled.

Ned remembered the funny look Suzi's father had given Roop's mother back on Spider Base. In a flash he guessed what was going on.

These two kids were them!

The girl was Roop's mother, and the boy was Suzi's father. As kids in 2069!

Nara pointed up to a small cave on a hill just beyond the crater. "Our folks are up there."

"Gran?" Suzi said. "Uh, I mean—"

Zeno stared at Suzi. "Have we met before?"

"Before?" Suzi gulped. "No, not before."

Ned edged to the rim of the crater and looked over the battlefield. He recognized the mountains from the images on the Spider Base dome.

"Cleaning your room is bad!" Roop blurted out, staring deep into Nara's eyes.

"Excuse me?" she said, pulling back.

"Well," Roop said, "how *do* you feel about, like, keeping your room clean?"

"I'm a very neat person."

"Bagel!" said Roop. "I'm too late."

BLAM! The sky erupted with explosions.

The kids ran for cover. Nara and Roop took off at the same time, dropped to their knees, and slid behind the crater wall.

Roop looked at Nara. "Nice slide."

Ned peeked over the crater rim and saw some kids fighting from the cave at the top of the mountain. They were firing at a squad of hinge-wings swooping down at them, while armies of aliens swarmed below and began to scale the cliffs.

"Guys, we've got to get in there!" said Ned.

Suddenly everything went quiet.

37

More than quiet. Everything went silent. All sound was sucked away, as if the air was made of thick cotton.

Ned struggled to cry out a warning. He knew what this meant. He tried to shout, but the moment he did, it was already too late.

"The *Wedge!*"

In a second it was there, Vorg's black time-ship, hovering above the crater rim. It landed in a spray of gray dust.

A ramp lowered from the ship, and a creature sprang down, half human, half spare parts.

"Vorg!" Ned gasped.

A dark creature in a long cloak, with a row of shiny bolts gleaming across his forehead, leaped at Ned.

"You!" growled the hideous creature, pointing directly at Ned with his ugly claw. A black visor stretched from one ear to the other. It sparked with red light. "You have hindered me for the past one hundred years! From the moment you entered my—"

Ned tensed with fear. "Wait, I—" But before he could say another word, Vorg pulled a silver ball from under his cloak and tossed it in the air.

A little red eye on the silver orbot flashed. *KA-ZAP—ZAP—ZAP!*

With each blast a hideous figure took shape. In no time a group of green, bumpy-faced aliens with long, rubbery breathing tubes and three slithery tongues apiece stood before them.

"Oh no!" cried Ned. "The evil Klenn!"

"You know these guys?" gasped Zeno.

"Yeah, we've met before!" cried Suzi.

HISSSSS! A foul-smelling snort went up from the aliens, filling the airless moon atmosphere with hazy brown stink.

Vorg pointed his claw at the kids. *"Steng-o!"* he cried out. Then he added, *"Hodd!"*

He stepped back into the *Wedge*, the engines roared, and he shot back over the battle zone.

HISSSSS! The Klenn snorted and stepped closer.

"What did he say to them?" Nara asked Ned.

"It's Klenn talk. It means 'Kill everyone!' "

Zap! The orbot swooped and blasted again, creating more Klenn. They charged.

Ned knew he had to stop that orbot. If he didn't, the whole crater would fill up with the slimy green guys. He dived to the ground, raised his stunner, and pulled the trigger.

Zwip! A cool blue ray zapped the orbot right in its flashing red eye.

Flunk! It dropped in the dust next to Ned's feet. It sputtered, spat a few times, then lay there, frozen in the dust.

HISSSSS! The Klenn edged closer.

Ned picked up the warm silver ball, popped it into his pocket, then scrambled to his feet.

Roop gave him a look. "Never mind the souvenirs, Ned. These dudes wanna *steng-o* us."

The Klenn stepped closer, surrounding the kids and pulling out their jagged swords.

Ned suddenly remembered a trick he'd seen his comic-book hero Zontar use against the Klenn in one of the early comics. "Act weird!"

"Excuse me?" said Roop.

"Be jerky," Ned urged. "Pretend to be loony!"

"Impossible," said Roop. "I am too cool!"

HISSSSS! The Klenn snorted, wagged their swords, and stomped closer.

"Tippy-ippy-yoooo!" cried Roop, dancing on one leg and waving his arms around.

It worked. The Klenn stopped. They looked at each other and began motioning toward Roop as if there was something wrong with him.

"First law of Klenns," shouted Ned, "is they're stupid!"

Roop kept dancing and waving his arms. "Way to think, brainboy!"

But that was just the first part of Ned's plan. "Now, time to tie up some loose ends!" While Roop kept dancing and waving his arms and the Klenn kept tilting their heads and pointing at him, Ned whispered his plan to the others.

"But won't that be yucky?" Nara asked, stepping back and making a face.

Ned shrugged. "Do we have a choice, Commander?"

"Huh?" said Nara, confused.

"Hey, slime guys," said Roop, "remember me?"

That was when Ned gave a signal, and Nara, Zeno, and Suzi crouched and then jumped straight up with all their strength.

Whoosh! The low gravity sent the Time Surfers soaring above the heads of the Klenn. In a single motion, they all reached down and grabbed the Klenn's slimy breathing tubes, yanked them up, and tied them in a snarly knot!

"Ugh!" yelped Nara. "This is disgusting!"

Green gunk oozed from the tubes as the kids squeezed and pulled on them.

"*Snelf!*" howled one ugly Klenn.

"*Floop!*" snorted another.

Ned held his breath. "Good thing we brought our own air!" he said, gasping.

The bumpy aliens struggled, but without their tubes they couldn't do much.

"Gulk! Noogh!"

One Klenn lost his balance trying to free his tube. In his panic he tumbled over and pulled the whole band of aliens with him. They toppled over the rim—a tangled mess of arms, legs, and slimy tubes rolling down the crater.

"Way to go, Time Surfers!" cried Roop.

In a flash the five kids scrambled back to the surfies. Nara and Zeno jumped in next to Ned, and they jetted off into the battle.

"Nice space car," said Zeno. "Is it new?"

"So new," said Ned, "it hasn't been invented yet!"

Blam! A sudden blast from Roop and Suzi brought down one of the robot-controlled hinge-wings. It collided with two others, and all three crashed in a distant crater.

Ned took out two more with some fancy flying and shooting. Nara was impressed. "You've done this before!"

"Those guys taught me everything I know," Ned said, pointing at Roop and Suzi.

Zeno nodded, watching the purple surfie do a triple backflip dive. "That Suzi seems cool."

"Hey!" shouted Roop from the screen in front of them. "Vorg's not staying for the show!"

"Our computer says he's heading into the past," added Suzi.

The *Wedge* circled the battle zone once and veered off over the mountain and into a blue timehole. Vorg was gone.

A moment later Ned saw a group of kids erecting a tiny flag on the mountaintop. It read KRONO CITY 2069.

"We did it!" shouted Ned. "Vorg didn't win!"

"We'll take it from here!" said Zeno.

"Good luck," said Ned, bringing the surfie down to the ground. "We've got some business to settle with that dude in the *Wedge*."

The purple surfie landed alongside, and Suzi popped out. "You guys are excellent!"

"You too," said Zeno, smiling at her. "Maybe we'll meet again?"

45

"Count on it!" Suzi answered. "And until then, remember, kids rule!"

"Hmmm," said Nara. "I like the way that sounds."

They all gave each other snap waves and—

VOOOOM! A nanosecond later the two surfies were going back.

Years and years back.

Into the past.

CHAPTER
✳ 5 ✳

Vorg's timeship had gone deep into time. The surfies were rocketing fast behind him.

"Score one for the Time Surfers!" said Roop. "We booted the dude out!"

Ned watched the years tick away on his surfie's computer. Twenty, thirty, forty years backward from the shadow wars. "He's not beaten yet, guys. Not by a long shot."

"I've tracked him!" Suzi exclaimed from the screen on the control panel in Ned's surfie. "He stopped in 2024!"

As they dived through a hairpin turn in the blue darkness, Ned turned to his onboard computer. "Bitzo, give me a total report—

big stuff that happens in 2024. What goes on?"

"Bloogball, sir," the surfie's onboard computer droned.

"Bloogball? What do you mean?"

"In solar year 2024, the Earth sport known as bloogball was invented by —"

"That's it!" cried Ned into the control panel. "Roop, Suzi! Bloogball!"

Suzi's face appeared on Ned's screen. "You think maybe Vorg doesn't like sports? And he's going to stop it from being invented?"

"There must be another reason why he stopped in 2024," Ned said. "Vorg's sole aim is to wipe out our future so that *his* future can happen."

"But bloogball?" asked Roop. "Maybe it's a mistake."

Ned nodded. "Or a trap!" For some reason, he felt sure that it would all make sense if only they got there on time. He gunned his engines, and his surfie blurred out ahead and into a steep downward turn.

Everything went dim and glimmery.

Next came the sounds of scraping, wrenching, cracking, and snapping.

"Hold on to your seats—we're landing!" cried Ned as the two surfies screeched to a stop and the kids went flying.

WHAMMMM!

Ned's face came smack up against a wall.

He opened his eyes.

A wall with pink and yellow flowers on it.

"Vorg's secret hideout?" he mumbled.

"You think maybe he has a soft side?" Suzi grumbled from the floor.

"Don't move!" said a voice.

Ned slowly scraped his face off the wall and turned. Crouched in a corner, clutching a silver ball, was a girl with long brown hair.

Ned felt a jolt of electricity hit his left side. He pushed his hand into his flight suit pocket. The orbot was in there. It felt hot. Ned felt hot, too.

"Don't be afraid," he began. "We came from the future."

"Oh, really?" said the girl. "I thought you came from my closet."

"Well, yeah, we did," said Ned. "But before that we were in the future. I mean, well, I'm from the past, but I was in the future, and then I went to the past, which is the present for you but it's still the future for me because I'm from even farther in the past, but if you come from the future-future, like my friends here, this is the present-past for them but not the past-past where I'm from, so this is still pretty much the future for me." Ned took a breath and wiped his forehead. "Can I sit down?"

The girl nodded warily. "I guess." She looked about the same age as the Time Surfers. "Are you really from the future? I've heard about it from my dad."

The room was filled with toys, books, and clothes. Next to the bed was a desk with a small red computer on it.

"Sorry for bombing your room," Roop said sheepishly, walking around. "I guess we made the wrong stop. Unless, uh ... you haven't seen a guy all dressed in black with shiny bolts in his head, have you?"

The girl suddenly leaped up and came over to them. She stared at Roop, wide-eyed. "Do you mean *Vorg*? You know *Vorg*?"

The Time Surfers all jumped. "How do you know about *him*?" asked Ned.

"My dad told me. He actually—"

Ned's legs felt wobbly. "Wait. Someone's coming!"

The girl raised her hand and stepped to the door. She put her ear against it.

"It's my dad!" she cried.

Ned, Roop, and Suzi all dived back into the closet.

When the door swung open, a spark of electricity shot across the room between the man standing in the doorway and the closet.

"Yikes!" whispered Ned, nearly fainting on Roop and Suzi. He felt weak and light-headed, as if he were going to be sick. "What's happening here? It's almost like the Zonk Zone!"

"It can't be!" Suzi whispered back. "There aren't two of you here. It's just this girl and her father. How could there be a Zonk Zone?"

"Maybe it's something you ate," said Roop. Ned put his ear to the closet door.

"Jenny," said her father, "Uncle Ernie and I are going to test the ball. Want to come?"

Ned slumped to the floor, feeling dizzy. He wiped his forehead again and listened. *Uncle Ernie?*

"Sure, Dad, and I've got a name for it," she said. "*Bloogball*, because it's a *laser-optic-omni-game ball.*"

"Hmmm," said her father. "That's *loogball*. What's the *b* stand for?"

"Our name, of course," said Jenny with a laugh. "Banks!"

A jolt of electricity shot through Ned. *Banks!* His own last name! His eyes widened. He shook his head slowly back and forth. "But how—"

"Zommo!" gasped Roop. "It's you out there! Can you believe it? *You* invented bloogball in 2024! This is sooooo cool." He stuck out his hand for Ned to shake.

"So cool? I'm being zonked here!"

"I'll be down in a minute," said Jenny. A moment later she opened the closet.

Ned pulled himself up from the floor and stared at her.

"I'm going to test this new ball with my dad and our neighbor Mr. Somers. Bye!"

She pressed a tiny button on the ball, and it shot up into the air and floated over her head. It circled her twice; then a tiny metal arm shot out and tapped her lightly on the shoulder.

"Point!" chirped the ball.

Jenny laughed, and in a flash she was gone, hopping down the stairs with the silver ball zooming after her.

"Wow! I almost got totally zonked," Ned groaned. Then he smiled. "She's really cool!"

"Of course she's cool," chuckled Roop. "She has an extra cool dad."

"Dad?" said Ned. His mouth dropped. "Does that mean that there is a— yuck!—mom, too?" He shivered.

"Guys, it doesn't look like Vorg is here,"

Suzi said, checking her Neddy. "We must have made a bad turn. Let's see if we can trace him."

Roop nodded, and they both disappeared into the closet to check the surfie's computers.

Ned heard voices from outside the house. He edged to the window to peek out.

There he was. Himself as a grown-up, a dad, yelling as he tumbled over on the lawn trying to dodge the zooming bloogball! And there was Ernie Somers, looking like a grown-up, too! He was laughing as the ball shot toward him.

"Cool, Ernie," Ned whispered to himself. "We're neighbors again. We still get to play!"

An instant later the bedroom door swung open and Jenny ran in, a look of horror on her face. "It's—it's—him!"

"Who?"

KA-WHOOM! A swirling black vortex coiled up out of nowhere and enveloped the room. The flowery walls disappeared.

And there he was, standing in the

swirling darkness as it sucked the room into itself.

Vorg.

Ned clutched the closet doorknob.

Jenny grabbed on to a bedpost. "Help!" she screamed, but the sound of the wind muffled her cry. Roop and Suzi were in the closet timehole. No one heard Jenny but Ned.

"Vorg!" he screamed out. "It's me you want! You can't have her! Take me!"

"Come!" He heard Vorg's voice echoing back through the horrible funnel.

Jenny struggled bravely to hold on, but her grasp was weakening. Ned knew what he had to do. He had no choice.

He let go of the doorknob and flew across the room into the vortex. It closed behind him.

To the rest of the world, Ned was gone.

CHAPTER
* 6 *

Ned whirled head over heels into the spinning darkness. He felt dizzy, as if he was on a carnival ride, spinning faster and faster until the floor dropped out.

All his muscles ached. His head felt like lead. His stomach was—

WUUUUUUUMMMMMP!

It ended as soon as it had begun.

Ned couldn't open his eyes right away. They were shut tight, as if they were glued together.

Where was he? *When* was he? He was afraid to find out.

As the black air slowly thinned, Ned

smelled something. Food. And not very good food. But there was something familiar about it. Then it hit him like yesterday's cold turkey cubes.

It *was* yesterday's cold turkey cubes! It was Lakewood School food. And it was all over him as he lay sprawled on the counter in the school kitchen.

"Pah!" He spat little bits of turkey and pimento out of his mouth.

He slid from the aluminum countertop onto the tile floor and shook food off his arms and head. The refrigerator door was open. He had come through the timehole in the refrigerator.

Why here? That was the big question.

Ned slung his stunner over his shoulder, tightened his utility belt, pushed on the doors that led into the cafeteria, and peeked in.

The big white cinder-block room was filled with people decorating the long lunch tables.

Cookies. Soda. Lemonade.

"Uh-oh!" Ned gasped. He pulled out his

communicator. The little screen read LAKE-WOOD SCHOOL, JUNE 29, 7:30 A.M.

"Today! This morning!"

Quietly he stepped in and began to walk toward the doors on the far side of the room. The main school hallway was outside.

Suddenly Mrs. Fensterman spotted him. "No sampling of treats," she said. She stopped. "Your clothes are . . . strange."

Ned looked down at his silver Time Surfer flight suit. "Um . . . my band uniform."

Then she noticed Ned's stunner.

"Saxophone," said Ned with a shrug.

"Ohhh." Mrs. Fensterman headed for another table, shaking her head.

Ned stepped out into the hall and tiptoed into the gym. It was empty, but it was set up for the big concert. He looked at the clock.

Wham!

The gym doors burst open, and a kid came in carrying an enormous tuba.

It's me! Ned thought. His senses jangled instantly. *He doesn't see me!*

Then it struck him what time it really was.

But by the time he got it, it was already happening.

Ned ran, dropped to his knees, and slid behind his other self just as he turned.

In a flash Ned pulled the tuba away from the kid, tripped him, and dropped the metal monster thing over his head.

Sparks exploded between Ned and his earlier self. He ached all over.

Two Neds! This was it! Zonk Zone time!

Jolts of electricity filled the air! Zapping him! Ned felt sick and weird. Really weird.

Suddenly it all made sense! Vorg had forced him to come back to this time and place, in order to destroy him once and for all. Sure, it made sense. Horrible sense.

All Vorg had to do was bring a couple of Neds together, and—*KA-BOOM!* Ultimate Zonk Zone! The result was simple.

No more Ned.

Earth becomes Vorgon.

Vorg rules!

"No! That can't happen. I've got to—"

That was when everything went strange.

The whole gym began to hum and crackle. Swirls of light flashed and flickered.

Ned watched his earlier self begin to fall and then stop. He just hung there, suspended over the floor, hands out, clutching at the air.

The clock on the wall stopped at 7:32.

"Time!" Ned gulped. "It stopped!"

At that very moment silence descended over the gym. Total and absolute silence. As if Ned's ears were stuffed with cotton.

As if there was no such thing as sound.

Ned felt the hairs on his neck twitch.

There was a soft rustling and sparking noise behind him. And the whirring of tiny motors.

Finally a voice, deep and gravelly, spoke.

"I have been waiting for you, Ned Banks."

Ice-cold chills ran up Ned's back and arms. He turned slowly.

Slowly, because it didn't matter how fast he went. Time didn't matter now. Ned was out of time.

Fresh out.

The dark figure stood motionless in the

corner of the gym. His black visor flashed red as he spoke. "You know why you are here."

The voice belonged to him. Vorg.

"Yes," said Ned. He knew. Vorg wanted only one thing—to rule the future. And Ned was always stopping him. All Vorg had to do was get Ned into the Zonk Zone.

And he'd done it.

Ned wiped his wet forehead. Every atom in him seemed to be knocking around.

"If you rule, you'll destroy the world," Ned said slowly. "Millions of people will die. Earth will be totally—"

"Mine!" growled Vorg. "I simply wait for the planet to cool and emerge to rule over a new planet. My planet. *Vorgon!*"

The whole gym went electric. The air was quivering. Ned felt sick and hot.

"In a little while, Ned Banks, you will be nothing but a handful of black ash!" Vorg growled. His growl sounded almost like laughter. "We have waited a hundred years for this!"

"We?" asked Ned. "Who's we?"

Wham! The gym door opened and in stepped Mr. Smott!

He wasn't frozen like everything else. He walked easily toward Ned.

"Mr. Smott!" cried Ned, running over. "Am I glad to see you! I know this is weird, but this creature is called Vorg. He's an evil time master and he's trying to take over the world. We have to call the police, quick!"

A flash of lightning zapped across the room from Mr. Smott to Vorg and back again.

Ned stared at the two of them. His brain wouldn't compute what he was seeing.

"Mr. Banks," said Mr. Smott, glaring down at him, his face lit up from the electric sparks in the room. "You travel in time."

Ned swallowed. "Y-Yes, but—"

"I found out," growled Vorg.

Ned turned to Vorg. "You? You . . . found . . . out?" He struggled to under-stand.

"I discovered your little yellow spaceship and went to the future," Vorg said.

"You?" said Ned.

"I discovered timeholes," added Mr. Smott. "I discovered power!"

"Wait a second," gasped Ned. "I don't get it! You always said time travel only happens in comic books!"

"So I thought, until I found your ship," Mr. Smott went on. "I became a being of the future."

"I became—Vorg!" said Vorg and Mr. Smott together. A jolt of blue lightning flamed between them.

"I can't believe this!" sputtered Ned, looking at his teacher. "All this time, you were him?"

"I became him," Mr. Smott said quietly, "because of you. That's the joke, Mr. Banks. You showed me the future!"

Ned felt faint, but Smott and Vorg seemed to get bigger and stronger with each blast of electricity that filled the room.

"Puny mortal!" growled Vorg, tapping the bolts on his forehead. "With these I harness the Zone's power. With these I have become—invincible!"

"But Mr. Smott!" Ned pleaded. "Remember about school, and kids, and tests, and stuff?"

Mr. Smott smiled. *"Ish poro-tu, Vorg."*

"Ta-fless noto, Smott," Vorg said.

Then Vorg whipped around, raised his claw toward Ned, and fired.

ZAAAP! Ned was hurled across the floor, closer to his other self. Sparks shot between the two boys. Ned winced in pain.

"Welcome to the Zonk Zone, Mr. Banks," snarled Mr. Smott. "In moments you'll start a chain reaction. All your atoms will begin to burst. You will explode. I shall control time. I shall rule!" He laughed as Ned had never heard Mr. Smott laugh before. "And to think the world believes I am only a teacher!"

ZAAAP!

Ned was pushed even closer to his other self.

It came down to split-second timing. He had to do something before he exploded into black dust.

ZAAAP!

"In moments," growled Vorg, "I will amass the largest army the galaxy has ever seen. I will begin my conquest of Earth right here. Right now. In my old school. Fitting, don't you think?"

Ned gasped for breath. He was getting weaker. Lightning bolts were flying between him and his other self, still hanging there, frozen.

Then it came to him. He had to bring time back. If only he had the strength.

"Sorry I've got to do this, pal," he whispered. With his last ounce of strength, Ned raised his stunner. He fired.

Ka-blam! A blue ray shot across the room and hit the tuba on his other self's head.

Bong! The time freeze shattered. The clock began to tick again.

"Ooof!" The first Ned crumbled to the floor. "Hey!" he groaned. "Who did that?"

"No!" shouted Vorg. He sprang toward the gym doors. And in that instant, that very second, a black funnel erupted from the stage and engulfed the entire room.

Ned's other self vanished in the whirlwind.

The huge darkness whipped up around Ned and lifted him off the ground. "No!" he cried. "I'm being pulled out of time! Got to save Earth!"

Ned struggled for his communicator. He pressed the green button.

Instantly hundreds of timeholes opened up in the swirling darkness. A thousand holes to a thousand different times and places.

Could he choose the right one?

Which timehole was his?

"Steng-o hodd!" screamed Vorg. A moment later an army of evil-smelling Klenn poured out of the whirlwind. They charged at Ned. The black funnel whipped around him like a tornado.

Then Ned heard a distant sound.

He knew it.

He dived!

CHAPTER
✳ 7 ✳

Floooook!

Ned burst from the timehole on the stage in the Lakewood School gym and shot right through the band rehearsal.

Saxophones, chairs, saxophones, music stands, saxophones, sheet music, and saxophones exploded out across the gym floor.

"*Nerrrrd?* What are you doing?" his sister, Carrie, shouted.

Ned stared at the kids making faces at him. "Where's Mr. Smott?"

"He went over to the stage just a second ago," said Carrie. "And by the way, it's the last day of school, not Halloween. Where did you get those weird pajamas?"

Ned looked down at his shiny flight suit. "Oh, man. I'll never live this down!"

HISSSSS!

"Ugh!" said another kid. "What's that smell?"

Ned thought quickly. "Gas leak!" he yelled. "Everybody outside!"

The kids screamed and ran for the door.

Ned stood alone in the gym.

The next instant a horde of Klenn burst from the timehole, their jagged swords waggling and waving as they stormed down to the gym floor. In seconds the gym was full of the creatures.

They snorted a horrible smell.

"Um," Ned said with a gulp, "slightly outnumbered!" He ran out to the parking lot. He knew that in a moment hundreds of Klenn would be swarming outside. They'd want kid shish kebab!

The kids were huddled next to the flagpole, waiting for the building to blow up.

"Aliens!" Ned cried. "But don't worry. I've

been to the future. I know how to deal with this. My stunner will stop these creeps in a second."

He stood his ground. He waited. He waited some more. No aliens. No creeps. No Klenn.

His sister turned to a friend. "See why I call him Nerd?" They all went back in the school.

Ned stood there alone. "No, really!" he yelled. "There are aliens! Green ones! All bumpy!"

At that moment the horde of Klenn burst from a side door and charged across the parking lot toward Ned.

"See, I told you!" yelped Ned, trying to run. "Aliens. And they're after me!"

All of a sudden—*ka-blam! Blam!* The ground around Ned exploded in a series of laser blasts. The Klenn snorted angrily and scattered. Ned looked up. Zooming down over the trees was a yellow surfie—his surfie! It skidded to a stop in the parking lot right next to him. The bubble top popped open, and out jumped—

"Ernie!" Ned shouted. He was dressed in a

flight suit with the Time Surfers emblem on the chest.

"Suzi and Roop blasted into my closet as I was leaving for school," Ernie said. "They thought you might need some help. I guess they were right. And I've got just the thing!"

Ernie pulled a small, shiny card from his pocket. It flashed in the sun. "A foil-embossed 3-D hologram card of our hero—Zontar!"

KLONK! HISSSSS! The Klenn gathered themselves and stomped closer.

"Um . . . got an orbot, I hope?" Ernie asked.

"I do," said Ned, pulling the silver ball from his pocket. It was cold. He rubbed it and flung it up in the air at the same time that Ernie tossed up the Zontar card.

Ka-zap-zap-zap! The silver ball spat out a ray and caught Ernie's card full-face. A cloud of smoke filled the air.

The Klenn stopped and watched as something heavy sprang up from the cloud.

"Zow-eeee!" cried a deep voice. "Klenn for

the stomping! And I thought I wasn't invited!"

It was him. Zontar of Zebra Force, in all his muscle-bound comic-book glory, flexing first one arm, then the other.

He grinned. "Them muscles! They just keep getting bigger and bigger!" He turned to Ned and Ernie and winked. "Stand back while I duke it out with the cover girls! Pee-yew!"

KLONK! The Klenn charged at Zontar.

HISSSSS! They stunk up the air.

"Whew! What you been eatin'?" snapped Zontar, holding his nose as he plowed into the Klenn, swinging his other fist like a wrecking ball. "Honk honk!" he said.

"Comin' through!"

He laughed as the green aliens jabbed him with their jagged swords. He bonked them and clonked them and finally stacked them in a big pile on the school steps.

The whole thing took less than a minute.

"Puny little fellas, really." Zontar sighed. "Not much of a contest."

Just then Ernie pointed to the baseball field beside the school. "Our troubles aren't over yet! Look, Ned!"

Ned saw a brownish cloud of stinky breath rise up over the ball field as another army of Klenn burst from the timehole behind the bleachers. "Oh, man!" he cried. "Vorg said he was creating the largest army in the galaxy—and they're all here!"

But that wasn't the worst part.

Cars were starting to pull up in the lot behind the field. People were coming for the concert. Ned saw a car he knew. A blue one. His mom and dad were in that car!

"Let's get down there!" Ned cried out. "Or my folks are bageled!"

CHAPTER
✳ 8 ✳

"Quick, Ernie! We'll cut through the school!" Ned yelled, slamming through the front doors and into the main hallway.

Ernie scrambled after him, leaving Zontar strutting around the pile of Klenn as if posing for photographs.

The hallways inside were cool and empty as the two Time Surfers ran side by side.

"Everyone's rehearsing in the gym," Ned said. "Or in the cafeteria getting the food ready."

"We had our party yesterday," Ernie told him.

They hit the corner at full speed and took a fast left.

"Lucky," grumbled Ned. He wasn't really thinking about parties, but he was thinking about luck. How sooner or later you ran out of it. Ned knew it was only luck that kept the whole time travel thing from really hurting somebody. But when he saw his mother and father pull up, Ned knew that his luck had run out.

When he pushed through the double doors at the end of the last hall and the midmorning sun flooded in at him, it struck him for the first time how very weird it was.

In the distance was the green summer grass, waving in the warm breeze that swept low across the baseball diamond. The sun was beating down hard.

Last day of school.

Last day of the world!

Because there, in that grass, behind the ball field, were hundreds of clomping, stomping, bloodthirsty, bumpy-faced aliens with only one thing on their minds—

Steng-o hodd!

"Okay, buddy," Ned said to Ernie. "We've got a job to do. Let's do it!"

Together Ned and Ernie stormed out onto the baseball field. They both knew that the game they were going to play was a deadly one.

A fight to the death.

The Klenn turned and charged, their heavy bodies thumping across the dusty field.

"Ernie, split up!" Ned cried, taking off toward home plate, trying to draw the Klenn away from the parking lot.

Ernie went wide and zipped over to second.

About a dozen aliens, their breathing tubes snorting and spitting in anger, pointed at Ned. *"Keesh-meta. Toof!"* one of them spat. Within seconds they had closed in on Ned, trapping him against the home plate backstop. He tried to inch his way out, but the jagged swords thrust in closer and closer.

"Back off, bad-breath dudes!" Ned yelled, but before he could raise his stunner, one ugly warrior flashed his jagged blade and knocked the device to the ground. It smashed into a hundred pieces.

"Hellllp!" Ned screamed, crouching down.

Whoosh! A flash of silver passed before Ned's eyes, glinting in the sun. The flash slid down through the jungle of falling blades, rolled under the legs of the Klenn, and crunched into the backstop next to Ned.

"Sorry I took so long," said Roop with a grin. "I stopped to munch a fripple!"

"Zommo!" yelled Ned. "Time Surfers to the rescue!"

Roop tossed Ned an extra stunner, and they began blasting away. When they were through, a dozen Klenn warriors hung in midair.

Ned scanned the smoky air over the field. Ernie was being pushed back to center field, completely surrounded by a ring of snorting Klenn. "Stay cool, Ern!" yelled Ned. "We're on our way!"

But before he could do a thing— *vrooosh!*— Suzi swooped low, her jet pack on full blast.

She reached down as Ernie reached up, snagged him, and shot away, leaving a crowd of Klenn swinging their swords in the dust.

"Wow," said Ned, watching the incredible rescue. "We are good!"

"It's like I always told you," said Roop. "Kids do everything."

Then—

KA-BLAM-BLAM-BLAM!

The shiny black *Wedge* appeared out of nowhere and dived at the ground, firing all the way!

CHAPTER
✳ 9 ✳

"To the skies!" yelled Roop, dodging the explosions all around him. "We can spray the Klenn better from up there!"

The Time Surfers leaped into their surfies just as the *Wedge* flipped back over the school for a second run.

Ned glanced out over Lakewood. He saw his house. His own window. The window he'd first flown out of in Roop and Suzi's purple surfie.

For that half second, Ned remembered all the good things that had happened since he'd moved to Lakewood. Roop and Suzi. The future. Time surfing. Incredible adventures with Ernie and his new friends.

And now, as he saw Ernie working the laser cannons and looked across at Roop and Suzi pulling alongside in their purple surfie, he knew his friends were with him.

Ka-blam! Blam! Ned zipped from behind a tree and blasted the field below. Burst after burst of laser fire drove the creatures back.

"Yes!" Ned cheered. Then he glimpsed his parents and other grown-ups walking from their cars into the school.

Ka-chong! The surfie shook. "It's Vorg!" cried Ernie. "He's got an itchy blaster finger!"

"And we'll scratch it for him!" yelled a voice from the screen in front of Ernie and Ned.

It was Suzi. She flew the purple surfie over the top of the gym and behind Vorg. Roop aimed the twin laser guns, and red rays sprayed out, nipping at the *Wedge*'s fins.

"Zommo!" yelled Ned as he circled over the school. But something caught his eye.

Another horde of Klenn burst up from the timehole behind the bleachers. In seconds they had blasted their way through the back doors and poured into the school.

"I've got to get down there!" Ned yelled. With lightning speed he twisted the surfie down through the trees, pulled up on the control stick, and skidded to a stop outside the back doors.

He leaped from the cockpit. "Ernie, you've got to get back up there to help Roop and Suzi. I've got to save my parents. And even Carrie, if I have to. I'm taking your stunner. Good luck!"

Ernie gave him a quick snap wave and powered off over the trees.

KLONK! KLONK! The Klenn were disappearing around the far corner when Ned pushed open the back doors and entered the school.

The gym! *That's where everyone is*, he thought. *That's where Smott is! And that's where the Klenn are heading!*

Ned ran down the empty hallway, passing classrooms and lockers on both sides, his eyes straight ahead. Action music began to pound in his head. *Bum-bum. Bum-bum.* Or was it his heart beating? He ran faster.

Ned gripped the two silver stunners hard as he spun around the corner into the main hallway. The Klenn were ahead of him. "Hey, stink-o heads!" he shouted.

The Klenn kept stomping toward the gym.

"Playing dumb, are you?" Ned squeezed the triggers of both stunners.

Zang! Zang! Zang!

The last row of ugly, bumpy-faced aliens stopped in midstep. They hung there, frozen.

Ned gritted his teeth and kept blasting.

Zang! Zang!

Finally the Klenn turned. They raised their jagged swords. *"Steng-o!"* one of them grunted. They charged Ned. He dived behind a water fountain and blasted again with both stunners. He needed to get past them before they got to the gym.

The Klenn kept up their charge. Ned dove ahead to the doorway of the teachers' lounge, crouched, and shot from there.

He stunned a dozen or so, each green alien instantly frozen as harmless as a statue.

"Time out for you!" Ned cried as he ran with all his strength to the main gym doors.

Bump-a-dump-a-dump-a!

The band was playing! They didn't know!

HISSSSS! The Klenn snorted and massed for their big attack on the gym. There were hundreds of them. They hunched together to make a wall. A stinky wall!

"No time left!" Ned exclaimed. He ran, dropped to his knees, and slid to a stop right outside the gym's double doors.

Ned set his stunners on megamaximum, took one last breath, and fired!

KA-ZAAAAAANG! The wall of frozen Klenn were blasted across the lobby and out the front doors of the school!

The force of the blast knocked Ned straight through the gym doors, past Mr. Smott at the podium, and up onto the stage!

"Ooof!" Ned flew headfirst into chairs and saxophones and finally right into the huge mouth of his own monster tuba! He finally breathed out—

Floooook!

The audience groaned at the sick note.

"Sorry," Ned muttered, pulling his head out of the tuba. "No time to practice!"

"Ish meta steng-o!" Mr. Smott screeched. His eyes flashed and his forehead wrinkled into a hideous frown. Suddenly he leaped onto the stage.

"Bagel!" cried Ned, scrambling off the far end and out a side door to the rear parking lot.

But just as he crashed into the open air, Vorg's *Wedge* came skidding across the baseball field!

It slowed and hovered in a cloud of dust over the pitcher's mound.

The two surfies skimmed the right-field baseline and landed nearby. The Time Surfers jumped out onto the field. Ned ran to them.

"What's Vorg doing?" Ned asked.

Before anyone could answer—*wham!*—the school doors banged open and Mr. Smott charged out toward the *Wedge*.

"Whoa!" said Roop. "The dude wants a ride."

All at once Mr. Smott whirled on the mound, whipped off his jacket, and jerked something shiny out. It glinted in the sunlight.

"His hand!" cried Ned. "It's— It's a claw! He's becoming Vorg!"

The teacher snarled at Ned. "We will triumph!" His voice was like gravel rolling around in a garbage can. Like Vorg's.

Zang! Laser fire sizzled across the field from Smott's claw. The Surfers dived just in time!

A moment later the *Wedge*'s ramp opened, and Mr. Smott strode up, lightning flashing and exploding between him and the dark time lord, Vorg.

A ray shot out from the *Wedge*. Hundreds of green Klenn quivered where they lay, went feathery, and vaporized into nothing.

Vrrrmp! The ramp closed on Mr. Smott.

"He's Vorg now," whispered Ned.

Vooom! Rockets thundered and the black timeship twisted across the sky and vanished into a distant timehole.

Ding-a-ling-a-ling! came the sound of the final class bell.

"Wow!" Ernie yelled. "School is over, Ned! Summer's here!"

"He'll be back," muttered Ned.

"He is back," said Suzi, pressing some buttons on her Neddy. "My vector search says he's going all the way back."

"When?" asked Ernie. "To the beginning of the school year?"

Suzi shook her head. "To the beginning of everything. Dinosaurs. Prehistoric time!"

Ned frowned, thinking about what Vorg might do in the past. "He isn't finished with us yet. Vorg still has plans."

"Come on, time dudes," Roop said, popping open the purple surfie and stepping in. "No use wasting time here. Vorg's up to no good, sometime, somewhere."

"Right," said Suzi, getting in next to him. "Besides, what are we doing this summer?"

Ernie looked at Ned. "I've got time. What about you?"

Ned looked at his watch. He smiled as he

climbed into the yellow surfie. "Time? Sure, we've got time. Lots of it. And I've got a feeling this mission is just beginning!"

"Zommo!" yelped Roop as both Ned and Suzi hit their surfies' twin thrusters.

With that—

KA-VOOOOM!

The four Time Surfers shot high over second base, twisted into hyperdrive, and headed for another mission.

Into the shimmering blue darkness of time!

DON'T MISS THE
TiME SURFERS'
NEXT ADVENTURE IN

SPLASH CRASH!
BY TONY ABBOTT

Coming soon!
Turn the page for an exciting preview. . . .

Excerpt copyright © 1997 by Robert T. Abbott
Published by Yearling Books
an imprint of Random House Children's Books
a division of Random House, Inc.,
New York

Originally published by Skylark Books in 1997

BLAM! BLAM! BLAM!

The black timeship's rear guns blasted again and again at the small yellow surfie on its tail.

BLAM! BLAM!

One explosion after another rocked the shimmering blue darkness of the timehole. The small yellow ship reeled back.

"Any more blasts like that and we're toasted!" screamed Ned Banks to his best friend, Ernie Somers, as a spray of sparks clouded their cockpit. Ned grabbed the control stick and plunged it to the floor, spinning his surfie into a tight turn.

"I'm on him!" yelled Ernie from beside Ned.

He pulled up on the firing arm and took aim. "All I need is one clean shot, and Vorg is cosmic pizza!"

"I'm pushing it to the limit!" Ned yelled back.

Suddenly a bright flash of purple zoomed up on their right side. Ned quickly glanced over to see Roop Johnson and Suzi Naguchi flying beside them in their purple surfie.

"The double Time Surfer whammy!" cried Ned. "Prepare to eat laser dust, Vorg!"

Ernie shot a look at Ned. "Is there such a thing as laser dust?"

Ned grinned. "Is there such a thing as cosmic pizza?"

"Don't get technical," Ernie answered. "When you're chasing down the baddest of the bad guys, sometimes you just have to wing it!"

Ned laughed. But he knew they had to stop Vorg. That was the number-one Time Surfer mission. A probe report had told them that the evil time master was up to his old tricks in Beta Sector. That meant it was a job for the Time Surfers.

Vorg wanted to control time for his own nasty purposes. Ned, Ernie, and their two friends from the year 2099 were official Time Surfers, dedicated to keeping the galaxy healthy.

Good Time Surfers versus evil time master. Simple.

BLAM! BLAM! The surfie rocked again.

Well, maybe not so simple.

As Vorg's black ship, the *Wedge*, twisted into a distant tunnel, a laser blast ripped past Ned's cockpit and shot into the timehole behind them.

"Be careful!" yelled Suzi, her face appearing on the screen in front of Ned. "Your teacher is still trying to teach you a lesson!"

"And he's handing out laser-powered report cards!" cried Roop from beside her.

That was the other thing about Vorg. The evil time master from the twenty-first century had actually turned out to be Mr. Smott, Ned's teacher!

He was mean, he was mad, and he didn't like Ned. At all.

And now Vorg was plummeting away into time. The Surfers didn't know where or when. They just knew they had to follow.

SHOOOOM! The timehole twisted and veered down and around. The *Wedge* plunged deeper and shot away.

"Keep on him, Sooz!" cried Roop. He reached for a small lever on the control panel. "Stick like glue no matter where he's going. I'm going to try to snag him with the magnetic tractor beam. We've got to keep time safe!"

Ned pulled up behind the purple surfie and followed Suzi's flight pattern turn for turn as the blue time tunnel deepened and darkened.

He thought back to the moment Mr. Smott had climbed into Vorg's ship. Electricity had blasted back and forth between the two of them until they became the same person.

Smott plus Vorg equaled Mega Vorg.

It was hard to get his brain around that.

BRONG! KROOONCH!

"Rapids!" shouted Suzi. "Vorg's heading for some bumpy territory. My vector readings are all crazy! We'll have to follow him in!" Suzi steered the small purple ship swiftly and neatly into the center of the timehole.

"Rapids?" said Ernie, adjusting his visor. "That sounds like fun!"

"Hold on!" shouted Ned. "We're flying blind now. We could end up anywhere in the universe, at any point in time."

Wump! Wump! Wump!

The yellow surfie bucked and shook as it rolled in behind Suzi and Roop's purple one.

"So we might not make it back for the cookout?" Ernie made a face. "I sure hope someone saves some burgers for me."

Ned had almost forgotten about that. Ernie was visiting Ned and his family for a few days. And they were having a cookout that night. *If* they made it back on time!

That was one thing about time travel. You could surf around for hours—even days—and then return to the exact moment you left. No one even missed you!

BLAM! BLAM! Energy blasts pierced the dark. Thick black smoke streaked the timehole.

"This is nutzoid!" shouted Roop, pulling the surfie's firing arm into position. "Scratch the magnetic tractor beam. We're fighting back!"

A battle in a timehole? That was dangerous. If their surfies were hit, it could mean instant destruction. But every blast they dodged could rip into the timehole itself, destroying it. And maybe destroying their chances of getting home.

Time travel was ultratricky. And major dangerous.

Vorg knew that, too.

Ned struggled to keep his friends' purple surfie in sight. He'd learned to control his own hypermodal antigravity warp-class chronoprojection surfer like a master. But his stomach was in knots. They were in totally unknown territory. Without their readings, they might not be able to get back home.

"Hyperthrusters!" cried Ned.

"On!" answered Ernie.

"Z-wing stabilizer jets!" said Ned.

"Locked on!" said Ernie.

BLAM! BLAM!

"The timehole!" screamed Suzi. "It's breaking up! It's breaking up!"

KRRKKKKKKKKK! A huge flap of timehole ripped open ahead of them.

Then Ned saw it. Beyond the tattered blue edges of the timehole was black space and nothing else. Just darkness.

"Hold on!" Ned said. "We're going up and out of the timehole!"

"Into what?" Ernie cried. "Where are we? *When* are we?"

Suddenly the black ax-shaped *Wedge* was there, coming at them from a side tunnel.

BLAM! BLAM! BLAM! Its lasers blasted again and again.

"We're hit!" Ernie shrieked.

The ship quaked and shuddered.

Then—*KA-BLAAAAAAAAAAAM!*

Everything went dark.

Bright light flooded the cockpit.

"Reverse thrusters!" Ned cried. "We're out of the timehole! We've got to slow down!" A huge sea of light blue water was suddenly below them, rushing up at tremendous speed.

"Can't!" yelled Ernie. "The thrusters are dead!"

Dead . . .

WHAM! The surfie's left side slammed into the water as if it was pavement. The ship hopped once, then skidded across the surface at four hundred miles an hour.

"Splash crash!" cried Ernie. "Hold on to your seat! We're going surfing!"

Wump! Wump! Wump! The surfie bumped across the waves at top speed.

"S-S-S-Somehow I thought it would b-b-b-be more fun than this!" Ned stammered as he was punched back and forth in his seat.

And then it got even less fun.

The surfie's nose dipped and caught the water.

FOING!

Suddenly the back end hurled up and over, flipping the surfie into a high-sailing somersault.

A somersault that ended too soon.

"Helllllllp!" both pilots screamed together.

SPLASH! The surfie hit the water cockpit first, bucked for a few feet, then stopped. *Ssss!* The red-hot engines sizzled when they hit the waves.

Ned's head hit the control panel. For a moment it seemed as if the light blue water all around them went black. Then Ned felt heat.

"Ernie, the extinguisher!" he screeched, pounding his best friend's arm. "Hurry, or we'll have our own personal cookout!" Bright white sparks were leaping from the control panel.

Ernie grabbed a small canister and sprayed the crackling control panel. The sparks died out.

Then water started pouring in through the cracked bubble top, and the surfie began to sink.

"Last one out is shark bait!" Ned cried as he whipped off his seat harness. Ernie hit the hatch release.

"It won't open!" Ernie yelled, banging on the release. "It's jammed!" The surfie sank deeper, bubbles rushing up around it.

Ned tried frantically to restart the engines. The surfie was going down swiftly. Water gushed into the cockpit.

"Thrusters are dead, forward jets are dead!" screamed Ned, flipping the top row of switches on the control panel. "And we're dead, too!"

Suddenly—

Nnnnnn! A rainbow of light shot through the blackening water and enveloped the ship.

The surfie jerked once and stopped sinking. It began to lift.

"What—" cried Ned as the sea around them churned and bubbled. "We're rising!" A moment later—*sploosh!*—Ned and Ernie's yellow surfie broke the surface, bobbed up, and began to slide across the waves toward Roop and Suzi's ship.

"Hooray!" said Ernie. "Saved by the Time Surfer magnetic tractor beam!"

Flonk! Their hatch popped open. Ned stuck his head out and shook the water from his eyes. "Thanks for the lift," he said with a grin. "We're soaked, but hey, we're alive."

The purple surfie was floating gently next to them. Its hatch was hanging open, too, and Suzi was sitting in the cockpit. She shot the two boys a small smile. "Our surfie's just barely alive. The tractor beam works, but that's about it."

"Excuse me!" came a voice from the other side of the surfie. "I'm turning into a fish over here!"

Suzi rolled her eyes. "Roop has a thing about oceans. And seas, and lakes, and rivers, and—"

Ned and Ernie jumped into the water and swam around the purple ship. They found Roop clinging to its side. "Guys, I surf in time, not water. I mean, hurl me in a time warp, crash me in the Zonk Zone, but just don't put me in water!"

Suzi took a deep breath and slid her visor to the top of her head. "We've got one broken tub toy here. Our navijets aren't functioning. We need some vacker units to get restarted."

"Ours isn't in great shape, either," said Ned. "Our controls are waterlogged and shorted out. And our thrusters—"

"Oh, no!" yelled Roop. "Fripples overboard! Our food supply is totally sogged out!" A half dozen of the doughy round treats Ned knew as bagels bobbed up and down as the waves carried them away.

It was then that Ned first noticed the beach. Soft white sand stretched for miles in both directions. The warm blue water behind him faded into the horizon. "Wow," he said. "I think we landed in a TV commercial."

"And here comes our rescue boat," said Ernie.

VRRRRR! An engine's roar drowned out the gentle sound of the waves lapping the surfies.

The Time Surfers turned to see a sleek black motorboat racing across the water toward them.

"Hey," said Roop, "a JetFin! Looks like we landed back in 2099! Wave them over—they can give us a lift."

A boy who looked about sixteen was standing at the controls of the boat. He wore a ripped red T-shirt and dirty jeans. His long hair was whipping behind him in the wind.

"Hey!" yelled Suzi. "We need help over here!"

But the black boat was already coming toward them. And it was coming much too fast.

"Is he going to stop or what?" said Roop, paddling away from the purple surfie and starting to swim for shore.

"I think the answer is *or what*!" said Ned.

RRRRR! The boat roared across the waves.

"Stop!" cried Suzi, waving her arms at the kid.

But he was aiming his boat right at the Time Surfers. Against his pale face, his eyes were like shiny blue marbles, glassy and dead.

"Dive!" cried Ned.

"Speed shoes!" yelled Roop, and the four friends hit switches on their flight shoes. *Whoosh!* Tiny silver jets ignited and shot the Surfers deep under the water's surface.

The motorboat roared over them. *Whack!* It smacked the yellow surfie, crunching a fin, and sped on as if it had never been there.

When the Time Surfers bobbed back up, the black boat was curving around an inlet in the beach. A moment later it was gone.

"What was *with* that kid?" sputtered Suzi. "He was trying to kill us!"

"Not what I'd call a rescue," mumbled Ernie.

"Right," said Roop. "With help like that, I'd rather swim. Come on. Let's get our ships out of the water before he tries to help us again."